JUNIOR BIOS

John Legend

BY NORA GARDINER

Enslow PUBLISHING

Please visit our website, www.enslow.com. For a free color catalog of all our high-quality books, call toll free 1-800-398-2504 or fax 1-877-980-4454.

Library of Congress Cataloging-in-Publication Data

Names: Gardiner, Nora, author.
Title: John Legend / Nora Gardiner.
Description: New York : Enslow Publishing, 2022. | Series: Junior bios | Includes index.
Identifiers: LCCN 2020035389 | ISBN 9781978522725 (library binding) | ISBN 9781978522701 (paperback) | ISBN 9781978522718 (6 pack) | ISBN 9781978522732 (ebook)
Subjects: LCSH: Legend, John—Juvenile literature. | Singers—United States—Biography—Juvenile literature. | Rhythm and blues musicians—United States—Biography—Juvenile literature.
Classification: LCC ML3930.L33 G37 2022 | DDC 782.42164092—dc23
LC record available at https://lccn.loc.gov/2020035389

First Edition

Published in 2022 by
Enslow Publishing
29 E. 21st Street
New York, NY 10010

Designer: Deanna Paternostro
Editor: Kate Mikoley

Photo credits: Cover, p. 1 (John Legend) David M. Benett/Contributor/Getty Images Entertainment/Getty Images; cover, p. 1 (photo frame) Aleksandr Andrushkiv/Shutterstock.com; marble texture used throughout HardtIllustrations/Shutterstock.com; lined paper texture used throughout Mtsaride/Shutterstock.com; watercolor texture used throughout solarbird/Shutterstock.com; p. 5 Berit Roald/Contributor/AFP/Getty Images; p. 7 Johnny Nunez/Contributor/WireImage/Getty Images; p. 9 Raymond Boyd/Contributor/Michael Ochs Archives/Getty Images; p. 11 Frank Micelotta/Staff/Getty Images Entertainment/Getty Images; p. 12 David Pomponio/Staff/FilmMagic/Getty Images; p. 15 Kevin Winter/Staff/Getty Images Entertainment/Getty Images; p. 17 Lester Cohen/Contributor/Getty Images Entertainment/Getty Images; p. 19 JC Olivera/Stringer/WireImage/Getty Images.

Printed in the United States of America

CPSIA compliance information: Batch #CSENS22: For further information contact Enslow Publishing, New York, New York, at 1-800-398-2504.

Contents

Words in the glossary appear in **bold** type the first time they are used in the text.

The Making of a Legend

When John Roger Stephens was born on December 28, 1978, in Springfield, Ohio, his parents probably didn't know he was going to be a child **prodigy**. They surely didn't know he would become the huge star he is today.

Who is John Roger Stephens? You likely know him as the piano-playing singer-songwriter named John Legend. He took on his stage name after a friend started calling him "Legend," a word that refers to a person known for doing something particularly well. John's music reminded the friend of the old legends of soul, a style of music that communicates deep emotions.

JOHN'S MUSIC MIXES SOUL AND R&B, OR RHYTHM AND BLUES, A TYPE OF MUSIC THAT COMBINES BLUES AND JAZZ. R&B AND SOUL WERE BOTH CREATED BY BLACK PEOPLE IN THE UNITED STATES AROUND THE EARLY- TO MID-1900S.

John's not the only musical person in his family. His mother, Phyllis, sang in and directed a church **choir**, while his father, Ronald, played drums at the church. His grandmother was involved in music too. In fact, John has said that she taught him a lot of what he knows about music. She played the organ at church.

FACTS BEHIND THE FIGURE

John's grandfather was the pastor at the church where John and his family members played music and sang. He says both the church and his musical family helped give him his start in music.

JOHN HAS TWO BROTHERS, RONALD AND VAUGHN ANTHONY. HE ALSO HAS A SISTER, MISSY.

John started taking piano lessons when he was just 4 years old. By the time he was 7, he was also singing in his church's choir. A few years later, he was leading the choir too!

Smart Star

John wasn't just a musical standout as a child—he was smart in school too! When he was younger, John was homeschooled by his mother. Later, at just 12 years old, John entered high school. Four years later, he graduated with the second-highest grades in his class. He was only 16 years old and two years younger than most of his classmates!

FACTS BEHIND THE FIGURE

When he was 10 years old, John became a spelling bee champion! He won the 1989 Springfield District Spelling Bee in his hometown, when he correctly spelled the word "**prejudice**."

JOHN WAS ABLE TO GRADUATE HIGH SCHOOL SO EARLY BECAUSE HE SKIPPED FIRST AND SEVENTH GRADES. EVEN THOUGH HE WAS GIFTED AT MUSIC, HE STILL WORKED HARD IN SCHOOL.

While he was working hard in school, John never let go of his love for music. In addition to making music at church, he performed in numerous bands throughout high school.

Meeting More Musicians

After finishing high school, John studied English at the University of Pennsylvania. As a student there, he led an **a cappella** group.

During college, John also worked as music director at a church in Scranton, Pennsylvania. His involvement at this church led to what some consider John's first big break into the music **industry**. John became friends with one of the singers in the church's choir who had grown up with a well-known musician named Lauryn Hill. The friend introduced John to Lauryn. After hearing him play piano and sing, Lauryn asked John to play piano on one of her songs.

JOHN WASN'T EVEN SURE HIS PIANO PLAYING WOULD MAKE IT ON LAURYN'S ALBUM. HE FOUND OUT IT DID WHEN SOMEONE CALLED HIM ASKING HOW TO SPELL HIS NAME FOR THE ALBUM **CREDITS**.

FACTS BEHIND THE FIGURE

The Lauryn Hill song John played piano on is called "Everything Is Everything." John was still in college when it came out. He has said he became known around the school for playing on the song.

JOHN MET KANYE THROUGH A FRIEND HE WAS LIVING WITH AT THE TIME WHO WAS KANYE'S COUSIN.

FACTS BEHIND THE FIGURE

After John met Kanye, the two worked on music together. John sang and played piano on Kanye's album *The College Dropout*.

After college, John moved to New York City, where he got a job working for a consulting group, which is a company that helps other businesses succeed. His dream job was to be a musician, but it can be hard to break into the industry and make money at it. Still, John never let go of his dream. At night, he played shows at local clubs. He also recorded some of his music and sold CDs he made at some of his shows.

During this time, John met many people who worked in the music industry. In 2001, he met another up-and-coming musician, Kanye West.

Gaining Grammys

In 2004, Kanye West started his own **record label**. Later that year, the label produced its first album, *Get Lifted* by John Legend. While John had recorded and sold his own albums in the past, this was his first album with a major record label. This meant it would be heard by many more people.

FACTS BEHIND THE FIGURE

Get Lifted includes a song called "It Don't Have to Change." Members of John's family, including his grandmother and siblings, are featured singing on the song.

GRAMMY AWARDS ARE A KIND OF HONOR GIVEN OUT EACH YEAR IN THE MUSIC INDUSTRY. WINNING A GRAMMY IS CONSIDERED ONE OF THE HIGHEST HONORS A MUSICIAN CAN ACHIEVE.

The album was also enjoyed and respected by many people! John earned eight Grammy Award **nominations** for the album. He won Best R&B Album and Best Male R&B Vocal Performance for his song "Ordinary People." John also won Best New Artist.

In 2006, John came out with his next album, *Once Again*. It helped him land his second Grammy for Best Male R&B Vocal Performance. In 2008, he came out with another album, *Evolver*.

In 2010, John and a band called the Roots came out with an album called *Wake Up!* When multiple musicians work together like this, it's called a collaboration. The album won three Grammys, including Best R&B Album.

In His Own Words

"I really just go in [to the studio] and try to create something beautiful and special and something that inspires me and hopefully will inspire other people."

IN 2016, JOHN CAME OUT WITH AN ALBUM CALLED *DARKNESS AND LIGHT*. THIS ALBUM INCLUDED COLLABORATIONS WITH ARTISTS SUCH AS MIGUEL AND CHANCE THE RAPPER.

Like his earlier albums, John's 2013 album, *Love in the Future*, was a big hit. It featured a song called "All of Me," which quickly shot to the top of the charts.

Who's Got an EGOT?

The four biggest awards in entertainment are the Emmys (TV), Grammys (music), Oscars (movies), and Tonys (theater). Winning all four, known as an EGOT, is rare.

For the 2014 movie *Selma*, John teamed up with the rapper Common to write and record a song called "Glory." This won the Oscar for best original song. In 2017, John helped produce a show on Broadway called *Jitney*, which won a Tony.

In 2018, John was in and helped produce a TV production of *Jesus Christ Superstar*. When it won an Emmy, John became one of 15 people to have achieved an EGOT. He was the first Black man to do so.

JOHN IS SHOWN HERE WITH HIS EMMY FOR *JESUS CHRIST SUPERSTAR*, THE AWARD THAT MADE HIM AN EGOT WINNER!

In His Own Words

"To have the chance to see your music be elevated and to have almost universally positive response to that music, makes me feel better every day. I feel more **confident** and inspired, and that's fun."

Even Bigger Things

In 2020, John released an album called *Bigger Love*, which he has said focuses on feelings like joy, love, and hope.

Even outside his music, John uses his fame to spread these kinds of positive feelings. He often works with groups that help people, gives money to charities, and speaks up for things he believes in. Some causes important to John are bettering the education system and ending **poverty**.

John has achieved numerous awards and is loved by countless fans. His career is proof that working hard and doing the right things can really pay off!

John's Timeline

1978: JOHN IS BORN ON DECEMBER 28.

1998: JOHN PLAYS PIANO ON LAURYN HILL'S SONG "EVERYTHING IS EVERYTHING."

2004: *GET LIFTED*, JOHN'S FIRST ALBUM ON A BIG RECORD LABEL, COMES OUT.

2005: JOHN WINS HIS FIRST OF MANY GRAMMYS.

2006: *ONCE AGAIN* COMES OUT.

2008: *EVOLVER* COMES OUT.

2010: JOHN RELEASES *WAKE UP!* WITH THE ROOTS.

2013: *LOVE IN THE FUTURE* COMES OUT.

2014: THE MOVIE *SELMA* FEATURES A SONG BY JOHN AND COMMON CALLED "GLORY," WHICH WINS AN OSCAR.

2016: JOHN RELEASES HIS NEXT ALBUM, *DARKNESS AND LIGHT*.

2017: JOHN WINS A TONY FOR THE BROADWAY SHOW *JITNEY*.

2018: JOHN WINS AN EMMY FOR *JESUS CHRIST SUPERSTAR*, EARNING HIM AN EGOT.

2019: JOHN BECOMES A COACH ON *THE VOICE*.

2020: *BIGGER LOVE* COMES OUT.

Glossary

a cappella Music made without instruments.
choir A group of singers, especially one that sings in a church.
confident Believing one can succeed.
credits A list of names of people who have worked on something.
industry A group of businesses or people providing a similar service.
nomination A suggestion for an honor.
poverty The state of being poor.
prejudice An unfair feeling of dislike for a person or group because of a characteristic such as race or religion.
prodigy A young person who is unusually talented at something.
record label A business that produces and sells music.

For More Information

Books

Lawson, Carlie. *John Legend*. Broomall, PA: Mason Crest, 2020.

McAneney, Caitie. *Gareth's Guide to Becoming a Pop Star*. New York, NY: Gareth Stevens Publishing, 2018.

Websites

John Legend
www.johnlegend.com/
Find all the latest news, including tour dates and new music, on John's official website.

John Legend Biography
www.biography.com/musician/john-legend
Learn more about John's life with this short biography.

Publisher's note to educators and parents: Our editors have carefully reviewed these websites to ensure that they are suitable for students. Many websites change frequently, however, and we cannot guarantee that a site's future contents will continue to meet our high standards of quality and educational value. Be advised that students should be closely supervised whenever they access the internet.

Index